The Fox and the Crow

Retold by Diane Marwood

Illustrated by Barbara Nascimbeni

W
FRANKLIN WATTS

KT-197-236

13
13
3

C153813748

First published in 2009 by
Franklin Watts
338 Euston Road
London
NW1 3BH

Franklin Watts Australia
Level 17/207 Kent Street
Sydney
NSW 2000

Text © Franklin Watts 2009
Illustration © Barbara Nascimbeni 2009

The rights of Diane Marwood to be identified as the
author and Barbara Nascimbeni as the illustrator of this Work
have been asserted in accordance with the Copyright,
Designs and Patents Act, 1988.

All rights reserved. No part of this publication may be
reproduced, stored in a retrieval system, or transmitted
in any form or by any means, electronic, mechanical,
photocopy, recording or otherwise, without the prior
written permission of the copyright owner.

A CIP catalogue record for this book is available
from the British Library.

ISBN 978 0 7496 8530 0 (hbk)
ISBN 978 0 7496 8536 2 (pbk)

Series Editor: Jackie Hamley
Series Advisor: Dr Hilary Minns
Series Designer: Peter Scoulding

Printed in China

Franklin Watts is a division of
Hachette Children's Books,
an Hachette Livre UK company.
www.hachettelivre.co.uk

KENT
LIBRARIES & ARCHIVES
C153813748

This kind of story is called a fable. It was written by a Greek author called Aesop over 2,500 years ago. Fables are stories that can teach something. Can you work out what the lesson in this fable might be?

One day, Crow sat in
a tree, holding some
food in her beak.

Fox saw her, and he wanted the food.

He thought of a clever way to get it.

"How beautiful you are, Crow!" he called, loudly.

9

"If your voice were as beautiful as you are, you would be the Queen of Birds."

Crow had always thought she was beautiful.

13

She thought her voice
was beautiful, too, so
she cawed loudly.

The food fell out of her beak ...

17

... and Fox
gobbled it up!

18

19

21

Put these pictures in the right order and tell the story!

vain

sly

silly

clever

Which words describe Crow
and which describe Fox?

Turn over for answers!

Notes for adults

TADPOLES are structured to provide support for newly independent readers. The stories may also be used by adults for sharing with young children.

Starting to read alone can be daunting. **TADPOLES** help by providing visual support and repeating words and phrases. These books will both develop confidence and encourage reading and rereading for pleasure.

If you are reading this book with a child, here are a few suggestions:

1. Make reading fun! Choose a time to read when you and the child are relaxed and have time to share the story.
2. Talk about the story before you start reading. Look at the cover and the blurb. What might the story be about? Why might the child like it?
3. Encourage the child to retell the story, using the jumbled picture puzzle as a starting point. Extend vocabulary with the matching words to characters puzzle.
4. Discuss the story and see if the child can relate it to their own experience, and perhaps think about the moral of the fable.
5. Give praise! Remember that small mistakes need not always be corrected.

Answers

Here is the correct order!
1. c   2. b   3. d   4. f   5. a   6. e

Words to describe Crow:
silly, vain

Words to describe Fox:
clever, sly